Dear
Welcon

Geronimo Stilton

THE RODENT'S GAZETTE
EDITORIAL STAFF

Geronimo Stilton
A learned and brainy
mouse; editor of
The Rodent's Gazette

Thea Stilton
Geronimo's sister and
special correspondent at
The Rodent's Gazette

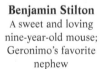

Trap Stilton
An awful joker;
Geronimo's cousin and
owner of the store
Cheap Junk for Less

Benjamin Stilton
A sweet and loving
nine-year-old mouse;
Geronimo's favorite
nephew

Geronimo Stilton

THE RACE ACROSS AMERICA

Scholastic Inc.

New York   Toronto   London   Auckland   Sydney

Mexico City   New Delhi   Hong Kong   Buenos Aires

No part of this publication may be reproduced, stored in a retrieval system, or transmitted in any form or by any means, electronic, mechanical, photocopying, recording, or otherwise, without written permission from the copyright holder. For information regarding permission, please contact: Atlantyca S.p.A., Via Leopardi 8, 20123 Milan, Italy; e-mail foreignrights@atlantyca.it, www.atlantyca.com.

ISBN 978-0-545-02137-1

Copyright © 2006 by Edizioni Piemme S.p.A., Via Tiziano 32, 20145 Milan, Italy.

International Rights © Atlantyca S.p.A.

English translation © 2009 by Atlantyca S.p.A.

GERONIMO STILTON names, characters, and related indicia are copyright, trademark, and exclusive license of Atlantyca S.p.A. All rights reserved. The moral right of the author has been asserted.

Based on an original idea by Elisabetta Dami.

www.geronimostilton.com

Published by Scholastic Inc., 557 Broadway, New York, NY 10012. SCHOLASTIC and associated logos are trademarks and/or registered trademarks of Scholastic Inc.

Stilton is the name of a famous English cheese. It is a registered trademark of the Stilton Cheese Makers' Association. For more information, go to www.stiltoncheese.com

Text by Geronimo Stilton
Original title *La corsa più pazza d'America!*
Cover by Giuseppe Ferrario
Illustrations by Danilo Barozzi, Francesco Castelli, and Christian Aliprandi
Graphics by Merenguita Gingermouse and Michela Battaglin

Special thanks to Beth Dunfey
Translated by Lidia Morson Tramontozzi
Interior design by Kay Petronio

28 27 26 25 24 23 22   17 18 19 20/0

Printed in the U.S.A.   40
First printing, April 2009

To: Geronimo Stilton

It had been a **stressful** day at the office. By six o'clock, I was exhausted!

As I scampered home, I thought about taking a nice, relaxing bath in a tub of **cheese-scented** bubbles. Ahhh . . .

Oops, I almost forgot to introduce myself! My name is Stilton, *Geronimo Stilton*. I am the publisher of the most famouse newspaper on Mouse Island, *The Rodent's Gazette*. I also love to read and write books.

When I arrived in front of my mouse hole at 8 Mouseford Lane, I noticed something unusual on the front stoop. Curious, I bent down to check it out. It was a package.

Could it be for me? I hoped so! I **love** getting packages in the mail.

I picked it up and *read* the tag. It *was* for me!

"Hmmm. Who could've left this here?" I wondered aloud.

I picked up the **B O X** and went inside.

To: Geronimo Stilton
8 Mouseford Lane
New Mouse City
Mouse Island 13131

Then I ripped off the brown **wrapping** paper.

Once I got the box open, I was dumbfounded and a little disappointed. Bicycle **HanDLeBaRs**?!

WHO HAD SENT THEM TO ME?

MORE IMPORTANT, WHAT WAS I GOING TO DO WITH BICYCLE HANDLEBARS?

You see, I'm hardly what you'd call a sportsmouse. My favorite hobby is *curling* up with a good book. So why would someone send me bicycle handlebars?

It was a **MYstE°Ry**.

TWO PEDALS?!

The next day, I woke up bright and early. I went into the bathroom and took a warm shower, just like always. Then I headed into the kitchen and got myself an apple and a nice cup of **HOT** cheddar, just like always. I left my house whistling, just like always, and headed to my office at *The Rodent's Gazette*.

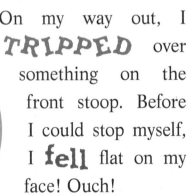

On my way out, I **TRIPPED** over something on the front stoop. Before I could stop myself, I **fell** flat on my face! Ouch!

I got up slowly, rubbing my tender snout.

That's when I realized I had tripped over another package.

I read the tag:

To: Geronimo Stilton
8 Mouseford Lane
New Mouse City
Mouse Island 13131
P.S. What are you waiting for? Open it now!

I decided to do as the tag said. I went back into my mouse hole and tore open the package. Inside were two bicycle pedals!

TWO PEDALS?!

WHO HAD LEFT THEM FOR ME?

MORE IMPORTANT, WHAT WAS I GOING TO DO WITH TWO BICYCLE PEDALS?

It was a conundrum.

A Bicycle Helmet?

I was still thinking about the two anonymouse packages as I headed toward my OFFICE. But as soon as I walked through the door to *The Rodent's Gazette*, my staff swarmed around me. There was no time to ponder the mystery. In fact, by the end of the day I had completely forgotten about the **WEIRD** gifts I had received.

Late that afternoon, I CHECKED the last page of *The Rodent's Gazette*, *signed* several important documents, and wrote a few chapters of my new book.

When I arrived at my mouse hole, I found yet **ANOTHER** package with the same tag!

I scurried inside and ripped open the package as fast as I could. By now, I was determined to get to the bottom of all this.

To: Geronimo Stilton
8 Mouseford Lane
New Mouse City
Mouse Island 13131
P.S. Open this package immediately, you cheesehead!

It was a bicycle **HeLMeT**.

WHO HAD LEFT IT FOR ME?

MORE IMPORTANT, WHAT WAS I GOING TO DO WITH A BICYCLE HELMET?

It was a puzzle.

As I mulled it over, the DOORBELL rang. I went to the door. "Who is it?" I called.

No one answered. But then the door BURST open!

I HOPE YOU LIKE
RIDING BICYCLES!

"Howdy, Geronimo! Happy to see me?" The mouse on the other side of the door gave me a hearty slap on the back. **Ouch!**

It was my friend **Bruce Hyena**. Bruce is the sportiest mouse I know.

"I've got a proposition for you, Geronimo," Bruce said. "It's something that needs LOTS and LOTS and **LOTS** of enthusiasm. You like riding bikes, right? If you do, slap me five!"

Timidly, I slapped him five. **YOW!** He slapped me so hard, my whole paw ached!

"I do like to ride bikes." I said. "I've got a really *nice* bicycle that has a wicker basket in the front. It's perfect for carrying a picnic and a book —"

"WICKER BASKET?!" Bruce said incredulously. "I meant a **RaCinG BiKe**, you **cheesehead**! You know, a serious bicycle — a bike for **real mice**! Not a bike for a *spin* in the park!"

I *smiled*. "Bruce, you know what a bookmouse I am. I like a quiet life."

"Quiet life? You'll have to squeak good-bye to that for a while! You see, I've already signed you up for the **RACE ACROSS AMERICA!**"

"The Race Across America?" I said blankly. "But that sounds like —"

"That's right! You bet!" Bruce interrupted.

"We'll be riding our bikes across the **WHOLE** country! No sweat, right?"

"But . . . but . . ." I sputtered. My head began to spin. "Rat-munching rattlesnakes! Do you know how big America is?"

"Of course I do!" cried Bruce, giving me another hearty slap on the back. "A trip like that should be a breeze for a couple of buff sportsmice like us, right, Champ?"

I opened my mouth to protest, but no sound came out. I think I was in shock.

Ha! Ha! Haaa!!!

My head began to spin, spin, spin, spin . . . spin, spin, spin, spin, spin

THE HISTORY OF THE BICYCLE

The first bicycle was invented in 1861 by the French mechanic Ernest Michaux. It was called the **velocipede**. The velocipede had pedals mounted on a large front wheel. This helped riders travel very fast with very little effort.

The **modern bicycle** was born in 1880 with the invention of the *chain*, which transfers power from the bicycle's pedals to its wheels. A few years later, **rubber tires** were added. Tires made riding a bike a lot more comfortable. Before they were invented, cyclists rode on wheels made of wood or iron.

Today **racing bicycles** have narrow tires, curved handlebars, and most important, a **gear** mechanism that makes it easier to pedal up even the steepest hills. These bikes are made from ultralight materials, like carbon fiber or titanium. Every piece of the bicycle is designed to be as light as possible to help improve the rider's speed.

What is the...
RACE ACROSS AMERICA?

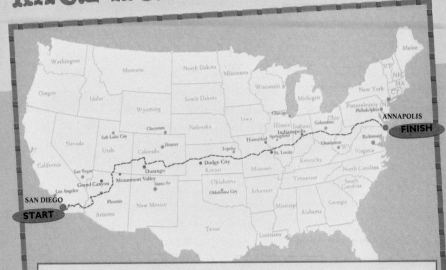

The Race Across America is the longest and most strenuous bicycle race in the world. It's an ultra-marathon race that's more than 3,000 miles long. Cyclists pedal for nine to twelve consecutive days, some resting only one to three hours every day. The race starts on the West Coast, near San Diego, California, and ends on the East Coast. The exact finish line changes from year to year, but was most recently in Annapolis, Maryland.

The race requires an incredible amount of physical energy, but mental concentration is also absolutely essential. In fact, some people believe that mental concentration is the most important factor in the race.

Cyclists climb more than 100,000 feet along the racecourse. Participants must pedal across the California and Arizona deserts, enduring brutal temperatures that can reach as high as 105 degrees Fahrenheit. Then racers must face the Rocky Mountains, the plains of Kansas, and the Appalachian Mountains on their way to the East Coast. It's easy to see why the Race Across America is considered one of the most difficult racing challenges in the world.

THE MOST CHALLENGING RACES IN THE WORLD

1. **The Race Across America** is a 3,000-mile bicycle race across the United States.

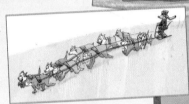

2. **The Vendée Globe** began in 1989. In this famous race, sailboats sail around the world without stopping. The race begins and ends in France.

3. **The Iditarod Trail Sled Dog Race** is an annual sled dog race in which mushers with teams of ten to sixteen dogs cross Alaska from east to west, covering 1,161 miles in eight to fifteen days.

4. **The Ironman World Championship** is the world's oldest, longest, and most prestigious triathlon. The first Ironman competition was held in Waikiki, Hawaii, on February 18, 1978. Competitors must swim 2.4 miles, bike 112 miles, and run 26.2 miles.

RECORDS FOR THE RACE ACROSS AMERICA

Riders can participate in the Race Across America as individuals or as part of a group. An individual cyclist can travel about 430 miles a day in approximately 22 hours. In the race's 26-year history, fewer than 200 solo cyclists have finished the race.

- In 1986, Pete Penseyres set a world record for biking 3,107 miles in 8 days, 9 hours, and 47 minutes.
- A cyclist burns an average of 300 calories an hour (a total of 7,000 calories a day) during the race!

UNCLE GERONIMO, YOU'RE MY HERO!

I didn't remember saying yes to Bruce's plan. But I must have, because the next day, he pulled up in his car and whisked me off to begin my 𝗧𝗿𝗮𝗶𝗻𝗶𝗻𝗴.

"But, Bruce, I have to go to work today," I protested. "I'm needed at *The Rodent's Gazette*!"

"NONSENSE!" Bruce shouted. He dragged me into a bike store.

Before I knew it, he'd bought me an outfit made especially for *racers*: a cycling shirt, shorts, socks, and special bicycle shoes that latched onto my bike's pedals.

"Okay, let's get going," Bruce

said. "I want you to meet the **TEAM** that'll be by our side throughout the **RACE**. They're all great rodents. You'll see."

Bruce stopped in front of *The Rodent's Gazette*. The entire staff was waiting for me. They all seemed to know I was going to be riding in the **RACE ACROSS AMERICA**, and they'd come out to show their support.

My cousin Trap, my sister, Thea, and my little nephew, Benjamin, were at the front of the crowd. Benjamin ran to *hug me*.

"Uncle Geronimo, Bruce told us you're going to **AMERICA** to race! You're my hero! When I grow up, I want to be just like you."

I DIDN'T KNOW WHAT TO SAY, SO I JUST HUGGED HIM CLOSE. What could I do? I couldn't DISAPPOINT my favorite nephew.

It looked like I'd have to race whether I wanted to or not!

N.M.C.
THE TEAM

Bruce took advantage of my moment of weakness to introduce me to the team.

"Hey there!" said a tall, thin mouse wearing a cowboy hat. "I'm **Tex**, the team's general manager. We've organized a system to monitor you at every step of the race. Put on these mini-microphones. They'll connect you to the camper that will follow you while you're racing."

Tex showed Bruce a tiny MICROPHONE that was attached to a long wire that extended from a small BATTERY.

"This way, if you need our help, we can get to you *FAST*," Tex explained.

Tex

TEAM N.M.C.

MOUSEY MACMOUSERSON
Known as the ranchero, Mousey is a cameraman planning to film the entire race for a documentary.

BUZZ
Buzz is Team N.M.C.'s mechanic. He's been crazy about bikes since he was nine years old. He runs a shop called The Bicyclist's Boutique.

SHORTY TAO
Bruce's cousin, a world karate champion. She works for *The Rodent's Gazette*.

TIGER
Our second van driver. A quiet, unassuming mouse like Geronimo.

NEW MOUSE CITY!

TACO ANDERSEN
Our second TV cameraman. He got his nickname because of his love of Mexican food.

TEX TALKINGTON
The team's general manager.

V-DOC
Our trainer. V-Doc is an expert at fixing sore muscles. All he has to do is take a quick look and he can tell exactly what the problem is.

IRONMOUSE
Our first driver. An athletic, well-rounded mouse who is also a triathlete.

MOUSITA MIDDLETON and BETTY SMARTMOUSE
Mousita and Betty work for *The Rodent's Gazette*. They organized the trip down to the teensiest, tiniest detail.

"Thanks, but I bet I won't need it," Bruce said. "I've been training for months."

Months? I gulped nervously.

Tex turned to me. "Sorry, Geronimo, but you'll have to carry an older version. We just gave out the last ultralight one."

"Oh, that's all right," I said. I wanted to show Bruce I could handle anything.

Then I saw the battery Tex wanted me to wear. IT WEIGHED AT LEAST SEVENTY-FIVE POUNDS!

Oh, what had I gotten myself into?!

"B . . . b . . . but how will I be able to carry this and pedal all those miles?" I stammered.

Bruce slapped my

"B . . . b . . . but how will I carry all this gear?"

shoulder. "DON'T WORRY, CHAMP. It's all part of training."

Training hadn't even begun, and I was already exhausted!

Tex smiled at me sympathetically. "You'll be just fine, Geronimo. Inside the camper we've got all kinds of things to help you rest and recover when you're not cycling. Plus our trainer, V-Doc, is the best!"

"Hmmm," V-Doc said thoughtfully. "Looks like I've got my work cut out for me! I can see you've got very small **MUSCLES**. Don't you worry, though. I'll fix you up in no time. Do you know what my motto is? *What doesn't bend gets broken!*"

I began to sweat.

Hmmm...

Before I could respond, Bruce had dragged me away to show me my bike. "Come on, Geronimo! Don't you want to meet your new best friend?" he said. "The two of you are going to be spending **A LOT OF TIME** together."

EVERYTHING YOU NEED TO TRAIN FOR BICYCLE RACING:

a helmet

a water bottle

a rain jacket

special bicycle shoes

energy food bars

a spare inner tube

a cell phone (you never know!)

tools to remove tires

a little money

Allen wrenches (always tighten all the screws on the bicycle before riding it)

GOOD FOR YOU, CHAMP!

Bruce showed me to my bike. It was a lot *fancier* than the one I used for picnicking in the park! It was sleek and silver.

"Come on, Champ! said Bruce. Let's take her for a spin to relax the paws."

That didn't sound so bad. I climbed on my new bike. Just sitting on it made me feel like a professional cyclist.

"Oh, I almost forgot to mention something," Bruce said. There are a few twenty-percent inclines on this course."

"Twenty percent? No sweat!" I replied enthusiastically. That sounded like nothing.

Bruce slapped my back so hard, he almost knocked me over. "Good for you, CHAMP!

We **PEDALED** for hours.

After 5 MILES, I was out of breath.

After 15 MILES, I had cramps in my paws.

After 25 MILES, my mouth was so dry, I had a hard time breathing.

After 50 MILES, my back was so sore, I wanted to scream.

After 75 MILES, I wanted to cry.

After 100 MILES, I fell off my bike!

Finally, we stopped for a break. "Bruce," I panted. "What does a twenty-percent incline mean?"

Bruce laughed. "Well, in bicycle racing, there are three types of inclines: the easy ones, the HARD ONES, and the **VERY HARD ONES**! A

After 5 miles

After 15 miles

After 25 miles

twenty-percent incline is **ONE OF THE HARDEST**. I thought you knew that, Geronimo!"

By the time we arrived  HOME , I was totally exhausted. Holey cheese, I couldn't wait to get off my bike.

I hopped off, but the straps that held my paws onto the pedals didn't release. **I toppled over** and landed right on my poor tail!

Bruce looked down at me. "You know what, Champ?" he said confidently. "Maybe I'll go for another **LITTLE RIDE**. I can't sleep if I don't ride at least a hundred and fifty miles."

He waved cheerfully and pedaled off.

Bruce Hyena is a good friend, but I'd never been so glad to see him go.

After 50 miles

After 75 miles

After 100 miles

►X

WHAT IF WE MOVE MR. X . . .

The two weeks of training were more **PAINFUL** than anything I could have imagined. But whenever I thought of giving up, I just remembered the look in Benjamin's eyes when he'd called me his hero and I kept at it.

Finally, the big day came. The entire N.M.C. **TEAM** was ready!

We met at New Mouse City's airport with our enormouse **SUITCASES**. We had to take apart our bikes and put them in special cases so they could fit on the plane.

We boarded the plane to find every seat was taken. The team was spread **ALL OvER thE PLACE**. That didn't

make Bruce happy at all. He was determined to sit **NEXT TO ME** so we could talk strategy!

"I'll ask somebody to switch seats with me," he offered.

"Oh, it's okay, Bruce," I said. I thought about the book I'd packed in my carry-on bag. I'd been so **BUSY** cycling, it felt like ages since I'd curled up with a good story.

"Listen, Champ, this may be our last chance to **BRAINSTORM** before the race," Bruce said. "We've got sixteen hours, and we're going to need every minute!"

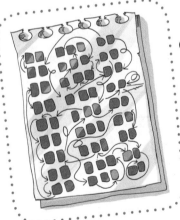

Bruce asked the mice on either side of both our seats to **switch** with one of us. But no one would do it. So Bruce pulled out a scrap of paper and started to figure out **ALL KINDS OF WAYS**

to move **RODENTS** around so we could sit together.

"Look, Geronimo! If we move Mr. X here, then we can switch Mrs. Y here and seat **21** will be ⓔⓜⓟⓣⓨ. Then we can ask Mr. Z to change with Mrs. H. Then there's Mr. Q, who will only sit in a window seat. Can you believe the n̈e̋RV̈e of that rodent?!"

Pretty soon, everyone on board was complaining about Bruce. The flight attendant had to tell him to take his seat and quiet down.

I breathed a sigh of relief and I pulled out the final *Ratty Potter* book. At last, some peace and quiet!

But not for long. After a few hours, Bruce appeared at my side. "Psst! Cheesehead!" he hissed. "Don't forget to keep your paws loose! Try these exercises."

EXERCISES TO STRETCH YOUR LIMBS WHILE FLYING

HEAD: Massage your temples.

EYES: Place your fingers on your eyelids and press gently.

NECK: Turn your head from right to left, then from left to right.

SHOULDERS: Raise your shoulders all the way up to your ears.

BACK: Bend your torso all the way to your knees.

ARMS: Bend one arm behind your head and push it down with the other.

FEET: First raise your toes, then your heels.

LEGS: Pull each knee toward you.

WAIST: Twist to the right, then to the left.

HOPE HOSPITAL

A few hours later I was starting to feel a little lonely. I peered around to look for my teammates. Bruce caught my eye and came over to talk to me.

"Geronimo, I've got something to tell you," he began. I'd never seen my cheerful friend look so SERIOUS!

"What is it, Bruce?" I asked. "You know you can tell me anything."

"Well, I've been volunteering for a while at Hope Hospital," he said. I was surprised. I had no idea he'd been volunteering. But it made sense. Bruce Hyena likes to talk big, and he has a big heart to match.

"I work in the wing where children with leukemia are hospitalized," Bruce went on.

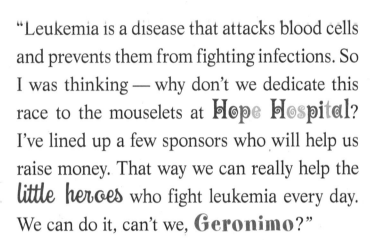

"Leukemia is a disease that attacks blood cells and prevents them from fighting infections. So I was thinking — why don't we dedicate this race to the mouselets at **Hope Hospital**? I've lined up a few sponsors who will help us raise money. That way we can really help the **little heroes** who fight leukemia every day. We can do it, can't we, **Geronimo**?"

I was truly moved. I hugged my friend warmly. "Bruce, that's a great idea. We can definitely do it!"

I CAN'T SLEEP!

Another hour went by. The lights were dim.
I looked around me. Everybody was sleeping.
Even Bruce was snoring!

I knew I needed to rest a little
before we landed. After all, I had
quite an adventure in front of me.
So I closed my eyes and tried to
doze off. But NO LUCK!

I called the flight attendant
and asked for a cup of **hot cheddar**, thinking
that would help relax me. But NO LUCK!

At the end of the flight, I looked frazzled,
and Bruce looked like he'd just returned from
a trip to the *Restful Rodent* spa.

It wasn't fair.

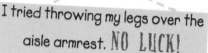

I tried crossing my legs. NO LUCK!

I tried putting down my head on the tray in front of me. NO LUCK!

I tried hugging my knees and resting my head on them. NO LUCK!

I tried throwing my legs over the aisle armrest. NO LUCK!

I tried curling up into a fur ball. NO LUCK!

I tried pushing my knees on the seat in front of me. NO LUCK! NO LUCK! NO LUCK!

WELCOME TO SAN DIEGO!

We landed in San Diego, **CALIFORNIA**.

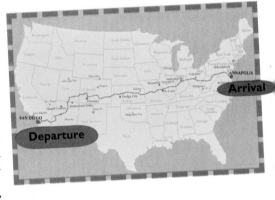

Arrival

Departure

I was totally zonked, and not just because I couldn't sleep. The **TIME DIFFERENCE** really made me feel terrible. You see, it was nine A.M. in San Diego, but back home in New Mouse City, it was **MIDNIGHT**!

As soon as we got to the hotel, **BUZZ**, the mechanic, immediately started putting our **bicycles** together.

While Buzz was **BUSY**, I figured

CALIFORNIA - SAN DIEGO

California is the third largest state in the United States, after Alaska and Texas. It is also the most populous. One of its largest cities is San Diego, which is located at the southern tip of the state on the Pacific coast.

The Spanish explorer Juan Rodríguez Cabrillo first sailed into San Diego Bay in 1542, hoping to find the wealthy cities known as Cibola. Today, if you walk along the waterfront, the Embarcadero, you will reach the Maritime Museum, which features one of the finest collections of historic ships in the world. One of the ships there, the *Star of India* (1863), is the world's oldest working ship.

In the heart of San Diego is Balboa Park. It is the largest urban cultural park in the United States. Founded in 1868, it is home to major museums, botanical gardens, performing arts centers, and the San Diego Zoo, which holds more than 4,000 animals.

I'd take a little ratnap in my room.

"GERONIMO! WHERE DO YOU THINK YOU'RE GOING!?" Bruce bellowed. He **BLOCKED** my path.

"Well, I had trouble sleeping on the plane, so I . . . I . . . thought . . ." I stammered.

"You thought you'd start the day with some solid training! Isn't that right? Good for you, Geronimo. I see the **FIRE** of enthusiasm in your **EYES**. I like it! Let's go for a nice jog."

Bruce is a mouse who knows what he wants and I could see that I wouldn't change his mind. So I dragged myself to my room to change into my tracksuit. Five minutes later, we were **RUNNING** along the waterfront.

Despite my exhaustion, being outdoors perked me up. **AH, CALIFORNIA!** The brilliant blue ocean seemed to stretch on forever. The seaside was gorgeous, with white sand that

sparkled in the warm sun. The beach was dotted with sunbathers and surfers.

It felt good to move my arms and legs again after being so cramped on that long flight. Bruce was right! Exercise was just what I needed. I **BOLTED** ahead, spurred on by the marvelous sights.

After a few minutes, I heard Bruce yelling, "... **nimo ... Wa ... out for ... ole!**"

I turned and shouted back, "What did you s — ?"

BANG!!! I ran smack into a pole!

Maybe jogging wasn't the best cure for jet lag, after all.

You Must Be the N.M.C. Crew!

Around **MIDMORNING**, the entire N.M.C. team gathered in our hotel lobby. We were on our way to the *CRUISE AMERICA CAMPING COMPANY* to pick up the camper the crew would use during the entire race.

Cruise America's owner, **MiCKeY**, was waiting for us at the door. "You must be the N.M.C. crew. I've got your camper right here. It's the last one left on the lot. You can sign the lease while I get the keys."

So Bruce *signed* the lease, and Mickey took us to our camper. It was enormouse, but it was dirty and dilapidated.

MiCKeY

TEAM N.M.C.'S CAMPER

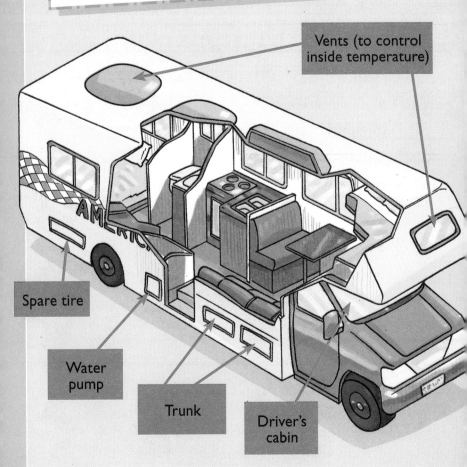

Vents (to control inside temperature)

Spare tire

Water pump

Trunk

Driver's cabin

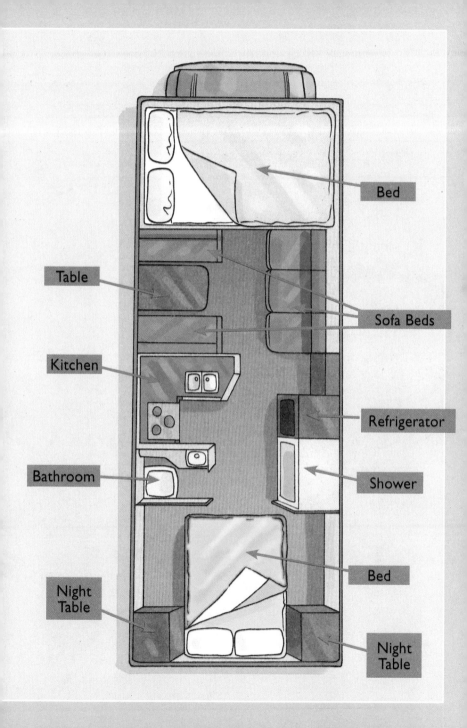

Bed

Table

Sofa Beds

Kitchen

Refrigerator

Bathroom

Shower

Bed

Night Table

Night Table

The rest of the team was as grossed out as I was. But Shorty Tao just said, "Okay, gang! With a little elbow grease, we can make this dump spick-and-span! So roll up your sleeves and get your tails in gear!"

We all went to work. We washed the floor. We scrubbed the counters and the walls. We shook, BEAT, and FLUFFED the mattresses, pillows, and anything else we could shake, beat, and fluff.

After everything was spotless, we aired out the entire place. Finally, we went to pick up some cheese for the trip. I was starving!

By the end of the day, I was wiped out. But the camper was ready to tackle the RACE ACROSS AMERICA, and after a good night's sleep, I'd be ready, too!

ON YOUR MARK, GET SET, GO!

The big day had finally come! I woke up, nervous but excited.

At the starting line, the atmosphere was ELECTRIFYING. Everyone was bustling about, checking their bikes, fitting their helmets, and making sure their water bottles were filled. Some of the contestants were looking over the route on **BIG MAPS**.

Bruce, **BUZZ**, and I were busy tuning up our bikes so they'd be in tip-top condition.

We **inflated** the tires, **greased** the chains, **TIGHTENED** the screws on our handlebars, and **ADJUSTED** the

seats so they were just right.

After the bikes were ready, V-Doc called us over. "Hey, Bruce! Geronimo! I'm going to give you guys a nice, **Relaxing** massage. Geronimo, you're first."

I scurried into the trailer. I love massages. But this turned out to be the least relaxing massage of my life! V-Doc *twisted* and **turned** me inside out, or at least that's what it felt like. By the time he was done, I could feel every muscle in my tail, and *not* in a good way.

Just as V-Doc started in on Bruce, we heard the loudsqueaker calling us to our places. No massage for Bruce, the lucky mouse! But I was too excited to care. It was time!

We put on our **helmets**. We'd decided I would **START** off the race. I was relieved because the first leg was the least difficult.

I joined the other cyclists at the starting line. Bruce slapped me on the back so

hard it was a miracle that I didn't fall over! "**READY, CHAMP?** Remember, pedal fast and smooth. Make sure you concentrate, and above all, keep a steady rhythm!"

I nodded. I couldn't believe the race was **FiNaLLY** beginning! I closed my eyes for a moment and thought about my dear nephew Benjamin, and how he'd said I was his **HERO**. I smiled and opened my eyes again. I was ready!

The voice on the loudsqueaker told us to mount our bikes.

"Ready? On your mark, get set,

GOOO!!!"

WELCOME TO ARIZONA

I had just begun pedaling when the rest of the contestants passed me in a flash. Rodents from all over the world had come to compete in this race. It was truly an international **event**. As we passed one another, we smiled and wished each other good luck.

The open road stretched in front of me. The wind whistled through my fur. What an adventure! For the next several days, I'd be sharing the same *destiny* as rodents from countries all over the world. Our hearts would beat the same rhythm of STRAIN AND PAIN. We would all share in the same excitement. It **was thrilling!**

As we started out, I felt good. Whatever V-Doc had done to my **muscles** had really helped. Plus, I had spent the last few weeks training with Bruce and the rest of our team, and I was in better shape than I'd ever been. And last but not least, I had *eaten* a hearty breakfast of **oatmeal** right before the race began. (Before exercising, it's good to eat a meal rich in carbohydrates.)

The **landscape** around me was breathtaking! I immediately settled into a steady pace. I smiled. I could hardly believe I was really here, competing in the **RACE ACROSS AMERICA!**

After a few hours, we turned onto *ROUTE 66*, the most famouse highway in the United States. I had already cycled almost 130 miles. In a little while, **Bruce** would switch with me.

As the sun started to sink, my paws began to ache. It was beginning to get **dark**. And I realized we'd entered the Arizona desert. There was a beautiful FULL MOON and nothing but sand for miles around!

ROUTE 66

Route 66 is the most famous highway in the United States. It was established in 1926 and is nicknamed the Mother Road. It begins in Chicago and ends in Los Angeles. Route 66 crosses eight states and runs for more than 2,000 miles. Jack Kerouac wrote about it in his famous book, *On the Road*. The highway was also immortalized in the song by Bobby Troupe, "(Get Your Kicks On) Route 66."

CHEER UP,
CHEESEHEAD!

I was getting HUNGRY, so I radioed **Tex** and **BUZZ**. They were following me in the team car. They pulled alongside me and handed me a cheddar sandwich.

Mmmm . . . cheese had never tasted so delicious! Biking hundreds of miles can really make a mouse hungry.

"Hey, Geronimo, is everything okay?" asked Tex. "You look tired."

"Just a bit," I replied. "I can ride a little farther."

"Do you need any more water?" Tex asked.

A **STRONG**, HOT WIND was blowing.

It was 105 degrees and it was nighttime! It was hot, but I didn't feel thirsty.

"No, I'm okay," I told Tex.

But a few minutes later, I knew I was in trouble. I hadn't followed V-Doc's **INSTRUCTIONS**. He had told me to be sure to drink plenty of **FLUIDS**. Suddenly, I had a terrible hot flash! My lips were parched, I was completely dehydrated, and I had a **HiGH FeVeR**.

Cheese slices! I felt really sick! *I must not have had enough water to drink.*

The team car suddenly appeared alongside me. Tex and Buzz must have noticed that I had slowed down.

"Take heart, Geronimo," Buzz said. "Bruce will **RELIEVE** you."

That's when I realized the camper was on my other side.

Bruce scampered out. He looked all *fired up* and ready to go. "Cheer up, Cheesehead, it's my turn now." He reached out to give me a slap on the back. And then everything went black.

I HAD FAINTED!

When I came to, the first thing I saw was **V-Doc**. He was bending over me.

"Geronimo, did you drink enough water?" he asked. "**NO, DON'T TELL ME! I DON'T**

WANT TO KNOW! YOU DIDN'T, DID YOU?"

I was mortified. I really didn't know what to say. I felt like a mouselet who had been caught with his paw in the **CHEESE JAR**. And now I was being scolded. But I hadn't done it on purpose, I had just forgotten!

V-Doc looked at me sternly. "Geronimo, because of your mistake, Bruce has been **PEDALING** for the last **EIGHT HOURS**!"

I was shocked. "Jumping gerbil babies!

I've been out for eight hours?"

V-Doc nodded. "Bruce knew you weren't feeling well, so he asked not to be relieved. He told me not to wake you."

I felt **TERRIBLE**. I couldn't believe I'd let my **FRIEND** down like that!

I had to do something. **I needed to**

Bruce after
TWO HOURS

Bruce after
FOUR HOURS

Bruce after
EIGHT HOURS

get well quickly so 1 could help Bruce!

"Please help me get better, V-Doc! I'll do whatever it takes."

V-Doc smiled. "**Good for you**, Geronimo. I knew you were tough! I'll give you a nice rubdown and you'll feel a lot better."

I had to do something.

My Turn!

V-Doc was right! As soon as he finished my MASSAGE, I felt ready for anything. I strapped on my gear and dashed to the front of the camper.

Ironmouse was behind the wheel. "Signal the mice in the car to pull over. I need to SWITCH with my friend!" I told him.

"Done, Geronimo!" Ironmouse said with a grin.

I put on my bike helmet. Once the camper pulled over at the curb, I jumped out.

Bruce had stopped a few feet ahead of me. He was taking a deep drink from his water bottle. He turned and gave me a tired smile.

"**HEY, CHAMP,**" he said slowly, "I'm glad you're feeling better!"

I hugged him. "Thank you for looking out for me, Bruce! You are a true friend. It's my turn now. So **SLAP ME FIVE** if you need to rest!"

Bruce grinned and slapped me five. I knew he must have been exhausted because it didn't hurt a bit.

I **WINKED** at him, then **JUMPED** on my bike and sped away.

THE GRAND CANYON!

I felt so much better. I pedaled mile after mile and I remembered to drink a lot of water. I was unstoppable!

Soon, **we arrived at the Grand Canyon.** Bruce was supposed to relieve me there, but I was determined to let him rest as long as possible. "I'll keep going," I told Tex. "Let Bruce rest a little longer!"

The road was filled with 20 percent inclines, but the view was **spectacular**. I should've been sweating my tail off, but the fantastic landscape made my aches disappear.

The walls of the canyons were very, very steep. Tex radioed and told me that some of the canyons were as much as a mile deep! The ridges were carved by thousands of years of ice, rain, and **WIND**.

I couldn't believe how lucky I was to be seeing this incredible place with my own eyes. Of course, it was very hard work, but the breathtaking panorama made it all worthwhile.

I really *owed* it all to my best friend Bruce Hyena. If he hadn't trained me like a drill sergeant, I would have never had the strength to take on those steep hills!

The Grand Canyon is a World Heritage Site in the state of Arizona. It is considered one of the wonders of the world. The canyon is a huge crack in a rock that averages 4,000 feet deep for its entire 277 miles. It is 6,000 feet deep at its deepest point and 15 miles wide at its widest point.

The canyon was formed by the path of the Colorado River over the past five or six million years. Over time, the canyon's walls grew wider and wider from summer thunderstorms and winter snowmelts.

The Colorado River cuts through the Grand Canyon. It begins in Rocky Mountain National Park, and flows approximately 1,450 miles to the Gulf of California in Mexico. Its waters change color from red to blue to green, depending on weather conditions and the different sediments in the riverbed.

Mousita

V-Doc

Buzz

Tex

Shorty Tao

Ironmouse

Tiger

Betty

As I zoomed along, I noticed a **CAMPER** by the side of the road. It was the **SWISS** crew.

My crew and I stopped to give them a paw. "What happened?" I asked.

The Swiss team manager looked anxious. "One of the camper's tires is **FLAT**," he replied. "If we don't change it fast, we'll have to pull out of the race!"

I turned toward Bruce and the rest of the crew. Everyone looked exhausted, but I could tell they knew what needed to be done.

Their **COURAGE**

and **determination** were inspiring.

"**All right, Rodents!** We've got the teamwork to make the dream work!" Bruce cried.

Faster than you can squeak "crumbling cheddar cheese crisps," we had that tire fixed, and the Swiss crew was ready to move! They thanked us **PROFUSELY**, and sped off.

"Okay, Champ, it's time to switch. You can't keep this rodent out of the rat race any longer!" Bruce exclaimed. He gave me one of

his famouse slaps on the back, and I almost fell over. **That's how I knew he was back to full strength.**

"Cheer up, Cheeseheads!" he told the rest of the team. "I feel stronger than ever. I'll fly over the next miles! Let's go!"

And with that, he was back on his bike and *RACING AWAY* as though all the cats on the Claw Islands were on his tail. He was more than a mile ahead of us before we caught up with him, and we were driving in the camper!

JUST LIKE THE OLD COWBOY MOVIES

I settled down in the camper's tiny kitchen for a nice snack. As I munched on a mozzarella ball, I looked out the window. We were in Monument Valley. The **red rocks** were bathed by the setting sun. What a beautiful sight! I felt like I was in an old **western**.

Buzz and I called Bruce on the radio.

"Howdy, partners!" Bruce shouted. I guess he shared my love of old cowboy movies. "It's very **WINDY** here. I can't go faster than fifteen miles an hour, even when I'm going downhill.

As we drove, Mousey and Taco, the two cameramen, had their cameras rolling, filming the **spectacular scenery**. And Bruce kept

ARIZONA
MONUMENT VALLEY

Monument Valley Navajo Tribal Park is 91,696 acres (143 square miles), and it's filled with many strange and unique sandstone

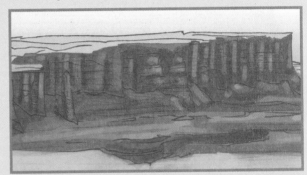

formations that have been shaped through time. They include buttes, mesas, canyons, and freestanding formations with enchanting names.

Ear of the Wind: If you listen carefully, you can hear the sound of the wind passing through the hole in this formation.

Eye of the Sun Arch: At a particular time of day, you can see the sun through the middle of the hole. It acts like a natural clock.

The most famous formations are the unmistakable Three Sisters, which appear in many Westerns.

SOME OF THE MOST FAMOUS WESTERNS OF ALL TIME WERE SHOT RIGHT IN MONUMENT VALLEY:

Stagecoach (1939)

My Darling Clementine (1946)

Fort Apache (1948)

She Wore a Yellow Ribbon (1949)

Rio Bravo (1950)

The Searchers (1956)

The Man Who Shot Liberty Valance (1962)

How the West Was Won (1982)

talking, even though he was still pedaling hard. He really is a mouse of steel. In fact, he started telling us j☺Kⓔs!

"Okay, listen to this one. There was a sportsmouse (just like me) who went to his friend, a bookmouse like Geronimo, and said, 'Want to do a marathon with me?' His friend asked, 'Hmm, how does it work?' So the sportsmouse explained, 'Well, we have to cover about twenty-six miles.' So the bookmouse squeaked, 'Fine, but you'll have to drive. I'm too tired!' Ha! Ha!"

I rolled my eyes. What can you do? That's Bruce for you!

FROM 120 DEGREES TO 40 DEGREES!

I lay down to sleep for a little while. It was important to rest while I could. I was so **exhausted**, I fell asleep as soon as my head hit the pillow! I woke a few hours later feeling rested and *refreshed*.

COLORADO

In the sixteenth century, Spanish explorers named the area Colorado because of its red-colored earth. Colorado means "red" in Spanish. Colorado has fifty-four mountain peaks that are more than 14,000 feet high.

Colorado National Monument preserves 32 square miles of canyons and mesas sculpted from years of erosion. A few miles west is Miracle Rock, a huge

sandstone outcropping perched on a narrow cliff. It may be the biggest wobbly rock in the world.

120 DEGREES

It was time for me to get back on my bike. Just my luck — we were right at the beginning of a huge mountain range. We had crossed the COLORADO border!

I'd gotten used to the heat in the desert, where it was 120 DEGREES Fahrenheit. But here in the mountains, the temperature dropped down to 40 DEGREES. Rat-munching rattlesnakes! It made the work of pedaling the bike twice as hard.

I panted and panted as I pushed one paw in front

40 DEGREES

of the other. Holey cheese, how I wished it was still Bruce's turn! The *steep* road up the Colorado mountains was more than **THIRTY-FIVE MILES** long! I thought it would never end.

As I huffed and puffed along, the weather suddenly turned from **SUNNY** to cloudy. *Brrrr!* Now it was even colder!

Just then . . . P**SSST!!!!**

I got a **flat tire**!

"Go, Geronimo!"

Before I even had a chance to radio the crew, **BUZZ** hopped out of the car and scampered over to me. Before you could squeak "chewy cheddar cheese chunks," he'd **FIXED** my tire!

HOW TO CHANGE A FLAT TIRE ON A BICYCLE

1. Remove the wheel from the bike.

2. Using an Allen wrench, carefully remove the outer tire. Then remove the inner tube and discard or patch it.

3. Take a new inner tube (or use your old, patched tube) and, after filling it with a little air from a bike pump, place it inside the rubber tire.

4. Insert the rim of the rubber tire back into the wheel.

5. Use your bike pump to fill the tire with air. Then place the wheel back onto the frame of the bike.

LAUGHTER IS THE BEST MEDICINE

After a while, we arrived in **DURANGO**, a beautiful town in the mountains. The landscape was dotted with pine trees and junipers.

As I pedaled through the city, a real old-fashioned **steam engine train** puffed by, tooting its whistle.

I was starting to get tired, so Bruce and I switched again. Now we were heading on toward **KANSAS**. It was hard to believe, but we were almost halfway through the race! The farther we biked, the more excited Bruce and I became, even though we were both worn out.

The crew was weary, too, and they were feeling a bit **down**. So I decided to try to lift everyone's spirits the same way Bruce had, which was by telling jokes. I'd had plenty of time to think some up while I was racing along on my bike.

My grandfather, William Shortpaws, was a big believer in the power of laughter.

When my sister, **THEA**, and I were little, he always used to tell us, "Remember, mouselets, if you feel down, the best medicine is **laughter!**"

Soon we were all laughing our tails off.

Why did the mouselet take his bike to bed with him? He didn't want to walk in his sleep!

Why can't elephants ride a bike? Because they don't have fingers to ring the bell!

Two mice are sitting in their yard one day. "I've really had it with my dog," squeaked the first mouse. "He'll chase anyone on a bike."
"What a drag," said the second mouse. "So what are you going to do about it?"
The first mouse shrugged. "Take away his bike!"

Ha! Ha! Ha!

Why can't a bicycle stand up by itself? Because it's two-tired!

Ha! Ha! Haaa!

Bruce heard the jokes through his headset, and he was laughing so hard, tears rolled down his snout. Even Tiger, who was driving the **CAMPER**, was doubled over with laughter.

All those chuckles and chortles made the next leg of the trip speed by. Soon we were in **DODGE CITY**, the heart of the Old West. Bruce had been riding his bike for several hours now, so it was **MY TURN AGAIN**.

DODGE CITY

DODGE CITY, KANSAS, WAS ONE OF THE MOST WELL-KNOWN CITIES IN THE OLD WEST. FOUNDED IN 1872, DODGE CITY WAS A MAJOR TRADING CENTER FOR TRAVELERS AND BUFFALO HUNTERS. TODAY, DODGE CITY HAS BEEN FAITHFULLY RECONSTRUCTED TO LOOK LIKE IT DID LONG AGO.

UPHILL STRUGGLES

Over the course of the race, I'd really started to enjoy riding at night. I spent the time plotting out my next few bestsellers. The gorgeous SCENERY really inspired a lot of great ideas! I was so busy BRAINSTORMING, I hardly noticed how hard I was working.

Sometimes I'd be so busy dreaming of books that I'd forget I wasn't really alone. Every once in a while, the mike connected to the camper would crackle.

"HEY, CHEESEHEAD, how's it going?" Bruce's

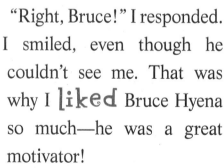
hearty voice boomed one evening.

Then Bruce grew serious. "Know what I was thinking, Geronimo? There have been so many enormouse hills in this race. That made me think of all the uphill struggles sick mouselets have to **Face** day after day. When you compare our struggles in this race to the ones the young mice at 𝕳𝖔𝖕𝖊 𝕳𝖔𝖘𝖕𝖎𝖙𝖆𝖑 are facing, it makes our hard work seem like nothing. If those mouselings can do it day after day, we can, too. Right, Champ?"

"Right, Bruce!" I responded. I smiled, even though he couldn't see me. That was why I liked Bruce Hyena so much—he was a great motivator!

PEDAL! PEDAL! PEDAL!

After a long night of pedaling, Bruce and I stood by the side of the road, getting ready to switch. Tex scampered up to us.

"Hey, you **road rats**. I was just on the radio with the organizers. There's only one TEAM ahead of us. And they're just sixty miles ahead! Do you know what that means?"

Bruce did. "**We can wiiiiinnn!**" he shouted. "Geronimo! We can do it! We've got to do it for all those mouselings at the hospital."

THERE WAS NO TIME TO LOSE! Bruce leaped on his bike and raced away.

Bruce and I became two lean, mean biking machines, switching every two hours.

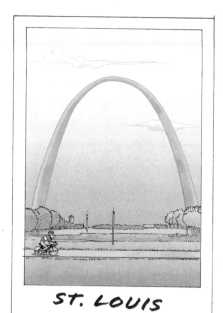

ST. LOUIS

The last few states flew by. When we reached St. Louis, Missouri, we saw an authentic riverboat docked on the Mississippi, right in front of the famouse high steel arch. Then we arrived in *Indianapolis*, where the Indy 500 takes place.

MISSISSIPPI RIVER

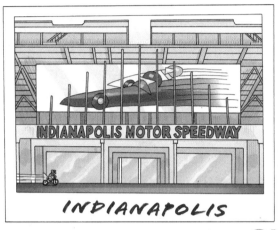

INDIANAPOLIS

Next we pedaled hard toward **OHIO**, concentrating on the rhythm we needed to overtake the racers ahead of us.

PEDAL! PEDAL! PEDAL!

OHIO

The distance **separating** us from the first-place team was getting shorter and shorter. Soon we were only a few miles from ANNAPOLIS, MARYLAND, where the finish line was waiting.

But just when I saw a sign that said ANNAPOLIS 20 MILES, something bad happened. Crusty kitty litter, it was **BAD**.

No, wait a minute. The word *bad* doesn't do justice to how **TERRIBLE** it was. It was awful. Ghastly, horrific, and dreadful. One might even say it was **DISASTROUS**!

It happened like this. I was pedaling along with Tex and Buzz behind me in the **team car**. At this point, we'd been pushing ourselves nonstop for more than twenty-four hours. And that's how Tex and Buzz turned onto the **WRONG** road without me noticing it.

No big deal, right? Well, the race's rules

say each team's car has to escort its cyclists to the finish line in **Annapolis**. Otherwise, that team is disqualified!

Geronimo ...

A BREATHLESS FINISH!

When I realized the car wasn't behind me anymore, I almost fainted. It's a good thing my shoe clips held me on the bike.

RANCID RAT HAIRS, WHAT COULD I DO? WHAT? WHAT

I turned the bicycle around as quickly as I could, Then I began *pedaling harder* than I ever had before. I didn't use the brakes once. I was like the wind!

I passed my crew in the camper. I'd radiocd them to tell them what had happened, and they'd stopped to cheer me on.

Bruce was standing outside the camper. He was cheering, "GO, GERONIMO! YOU CAN DO IT!!!"

Finally, I saw a dot faraway on the horizon. It was coming toward me. It was our team car.

"Go, Geronimo, go!" Tex shouted.

Faster than you can squeak "flying cheese sticks dipped in fondue," I'd turned around and started sprinting in the OPPOSITE DIRECTION. We were back on track and heading toward the FINISH line!

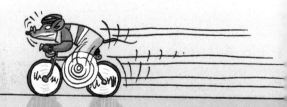

I'd never pedaled faster in my life.

My mouth was **dry**, my paws were **ACHING**, and sweat was dripping down my fur right into my eyes.

But there it was! The FINISH line! And there, just a few yards away from it, was the cyclist from the team ahead of us!

I was so close, I knew I could catch up with him. This was the FINAL STRETCH! There were all the fans! There was my crew about to cross the FINISH line!

At that moment, I tried to accelerate, but my front tire hit a rock and . . .

Suddenly, I was **FLYiNGGGGGGG!!!!!!!!!**

FRIENDS TOGETHER!
MICE FOREVER!

Here's what happened next.

Because of that rock, I **FLIPPED** through the air and landed right on top of my opponent's head. Then I **tumbled** onto the FINISH line! That flying leap onto the FINISH line helped me finish first!

WE HAD WOOOOOOOOOOOOOOON!!!!

Bruce and the entire team ran to hug me. They were so thrilled it ended up being more of a tackle than a hug. Soon the whole team was piled on top of me. But I didn't care.

"Yeaaaah!" shrieked Tex. "We did it!"

Bruce was hugging me so hard, I thought he was going to crush my ribs. "Cheesehead, when I told you the trick to **winning** was to arrive a second before the rodent in first place, I never thought you'd take me literally!" He gave me another tail-crunching embrace. "You really *are* a champ now!"

We **hugged** each other. Then I turned and embraced all the members of our crew one by one. This victory was for everybody, not just for Bruce and me. We never could have done it without our team.

At the AWARDS CEREMONY, we called the whole crew onto the stand with us to receive the trophy — Shorty Tao, Betty,

Mousita, Tex, V-Doc, Ironmouse, Tiger, Taco, Mousey, and Buzz!

Bruce winked at me. "You know, Geronimo, it took more than muscles to win this race. It took heart. And we've got lots of that on this team!"

I grinned at him. Then we joined hands with our teammates and shouted an old New Mouse City motto: *"Friends together! Mice forever!"*

HEY, CHEESEHEAD, ARE YOU SLEEPING?

That night, we had a **BIG** dinner to celebrate our victory. The next morning, we all boarded the plane for the flight back to New Mouse City. I couldn't wait to get home and tell Benjamin, Thea, and Trap all about our adventure.

"PSST! PSST! HEY, CHEESEHEAD!" Bruce whispered. "Slap me five if you're sleeping!"

I **rolled** my eyes. "Bruce, how I can slap you five if I'm really **sleeping**?"

"Good for you, Champ! I always knew you were a **BRainy** mouse!"

Psst! Psst!

I smiled at him, then leaned my snout against my seat and tried to fall asleep.

I closed my eyes. In just a few hours, I'd be home in my nice, cozy mouse hole.

"PSST! PSST! HEY, CHEESEHEAD, ARE YOU SLEEPING?"

This time, I couldn't take it. "NO, I'M NOT SLEEPING! YOU WON'T LET ME!"

Uh-oh. I'd woken up the whole plane! And they were angrier than a mouse whose cheese has gone moldy.

"Shhhhh!"

"Who taught you your manners? A rabid tomcat?!"

"Be quiet!"

I was so EMBARRASSED, I wanted to crawl under my seat!

Bruce just ignored everyone and leaned

in closer. "Well, since you're not sleeping, I was thinking of something. What do you say about organizing another fun ADVENTURE with me? I've got a bunch of great ideas. How about a MOUNTAIN BIKE trip through Patagonia? Or

a trek through the Valley of the Dinosaurs? Or we could do a nice little RUN up to the North Pole? Huh? What do you think?"

I had to laugh. "Just thinking about all those trips is making me tired, Bruce. Good night!"

THE REAL HEROES!

"Hey there, cousin!"

"Congratulations!"

"Uncle G!"

When our plane landed in New Mouse City, my entire **family** was waiting for me at the airport. In fact, half of New Mouse City had turned out to welcome us.

I WAS SO HAPPY TO BE HOME!

Benjamin jumped up to hug me. "Uncle G, I knew you could do it! **I LOVE YOU SO MUCH!**"

I kissed the tips of his whiskers, then gave him a tight squeeze.

My sister gave me a big hug. "I'm so proud

of you, Gerry Berry," she whispered.

Even my prankster cousin Trap looked happy to see me. I could tell he was busy trying to think up jokes to make — at my expense, of course. So before he could squeak, I gave him a Bruce-style slap on the back. That surprised him into silence!

I wanted to go straight home, but Bruce insisted we go to Hope Hospital first. And I was glad he did, because all the sick mouselings to whom we had dedicated our victory were waiting for us. They welcomed us like we were real heroes. But the fact was, *they* were the real heroes! That's why Bruce and I decided to give our little friends our trophy. Those mouselets were the ones who showed us real courage: the courage to face life!

Even though they were sick, these young mice found the strength to keep GOING.

They never let their suffering bring them down. For these young mice, every day was a new day, rich with **possibilities**.

Bruce presented the hospital administrator with a check for all the money we'd raised. I could see tears shining in her eyes. She looked so happy.

Looking at the *smiles* on those mouselets' snouts made me feel great. The RACE ACROSS AMERICA had been an enormouse challenge for me, but it was worth it. Bruce and I had an amazing adventure, and we were able to help some very special little mouselets. Given the chance, I knew I would do it again in a heartbeat!

THEA STILTON AND THE DRAGON'S CODE

I couldn't believe it when I, Thea Stilton, was invited to teach a journalism class at Mouse Island's most prestigious university! I had no idea that once I arrived, I would meet five amazing students. What's more, I didn't realize that another student would disappear—and the rest of us would have to help solve the mystery! Holey Swiss cheese, it was an incredible adventure!

And don't miss any of my other fabumouse adventures!

#1 LOST TREASURE OF THE EMERALD EYE

#2 THE CURSE OF THE CHEESE PYRAMID

#3 CAT AND MOUSE IN A HAUNTED HOUSE

#4 I'M TOO FOND OF MY FUR!

#5 FOUR MICE DEEP IN THE JUNGLE

#6 PAWS OFF, CHEDDARFACE!

#7 RED PIZZAS FOR A BLUE COUNT

#8 ATTACK OF THE BANDIT CATS

#9 A FABUMOUSE VACATION FOR GERONIMO

#10 ALL BECAUSE OF A CUP OF COFFEE

#11 IT'S HALLOWEEN, YOU 'FRAIDY MOUSE!

#12 MERRY CHRISTMAS, GERONIMO!

#13 THE PHANTOM OF THE SUBWAY

#14 THE TEMPLE OF THE RUBY OF FIRE

#15 THE MONA MOUSA CODE

#16 A CHEESE-COLORED CAMPER

#17 WATCH YOUR WHISKERS, STILTON!

#18 SHIPWRECK ON THE PIRATE ISLANDS

#19 MY NAME IS STILTON, GERONIMO STILTON

#20 SURF'S UP, GERONIMO!

#21 THE WILD, WILD WEST

#22 THE SECRET OF CACKLEFUR CASTLE

A CHRISTMAS TALE

#23 VALENTINE'S DAY DISASTER

#24 FIELD TRIP TO NIAGARA FALLS

#25 THE SEARCH FOR SUNKEN TREASURE

#26 THE MUMMY WITH NO NAME

#27 THE CHRISTMAS TOY FACTORY

#28 WEDDING CRASHER

#29 DOWN AND OUT DOWN UNDER

#30 THE MOUSE ISLAND MARATHON

#31 THE MYSTERIOUS CHEESE THIEF

CHRISTMAS CATASTROPHE

#32 VALLEY OF THE GIANT SKELETONS

#33 GERONIMO AND THE GOLD MEDAL MYSTERY

#34 GERONIMO STILTON, SECRET AGENT

#35 A VERY MERRY CHRISTMAS

#36 GERONIMO'S VALENTINE

And don't forget to look for

THEA STILTON AND THE DRAGON'S CODE

ABOUT THE AUTHOR

Born in New Mouse City, Mouse Island, Geronimo Stilton is Rattus Emeritus of Mousomorphic Literature and of Neo-Ratonic Comparative Philosophy. For the past twenty years, he has been running *The Rodent's Gazette*, New Mouse City's most widely read daily newspaper.

Stilton was awarded the Ratitzer Prize for his scoops on *The Curse of the Cheese Pyramid* and *The Search for Sunken Treasure*. He has also received the Andersen 2000 Prize for Personality of the Year. One of his bestsellers won the 2002 eBook Award for world's best ratlings' electronic book. His works have been published all over the globe.

In his spare time, Mr. Stilton collects antique cheese rinds and plays golf. But what he most enjoys is telling stories to his nephew Benjamin.

THE RODENT'S GAZETTE

1. Main entrance
2. Printing presses (where the books and newspaper are printed)
3. Accounts department
4. Editorial room (where the editors, illustrators, and designers work)
5. Geronimo Stilton's office
6. Storage space for Geronimo's books

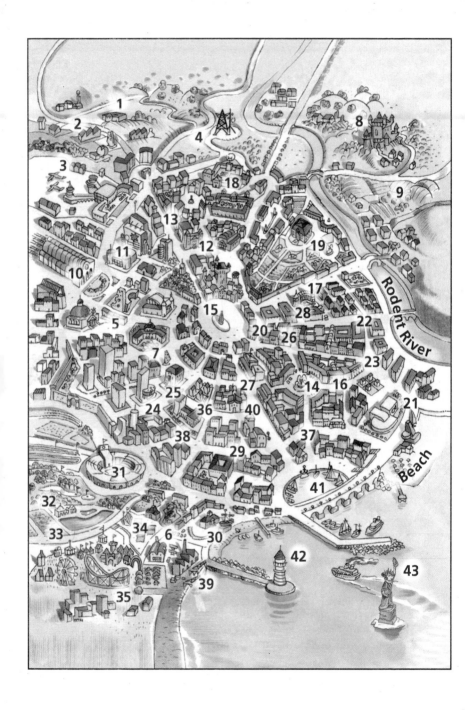

Map of New Mouse City

1. Industrial Zone
2. Cheese Factories
3. Angorat International Airport
4. WRAT Radio and Television Station
5. Cheese Market
6. Fish Market
7. Town Hall
8. Snotnose Castle
9. The Seven Hills of Mouse Island
10. Mouse Central Station
11. Trade Center
12. Movie Theater
13. Gym
14. Catnegie Hall
15. Singing Stone Plaza
16. The Gouda Theater
17. Grand Hotel
18. Mouse General Hospital
19. Botanical Gardens
20. Cheap Junk for Less (Trap's store)
21. Parking Lot
22. Mouseum of Modern Art
23. University and Library
24. *The Daily Rat*
25. *The Rodent's Gazette*
26. Trap's House
27. Fashion District
28. The Mouse House Restaurant
29. Environmental Protection Center
30. Harbor Office
31. Mousidon Square Garden
32. Golf Course
33. Swimming Pool
34. Blushing Meadow Tennis Courts
35. Curlyfur Island Amusement Park
36. Geronimo's House
37. New Mouse City Historic District
38. Public Library
39. Shipyard
40. Thea's House
41. New Mouse Harbor
42. Luna Lighthouse
43. The Statue of Liberty

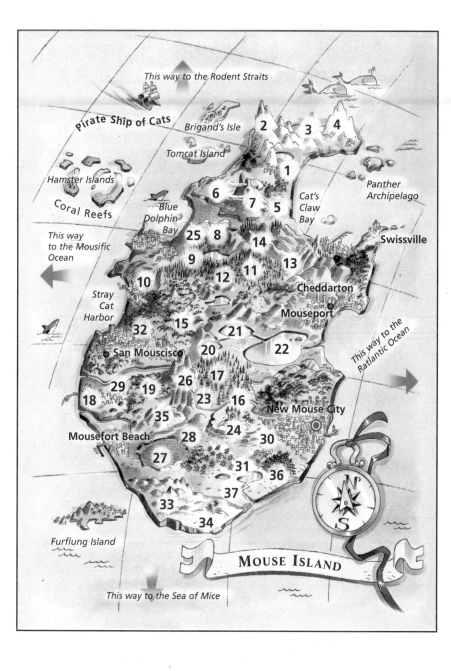

Map of Mouse Island

1. Big Ice Lake
2. Frozen Fur Peak
3. Slipperyslopes Glacier
4. Coldcreeps Peak
5. Ratzikistan
6. Transratania
7. Mount Vamp
8. Roastedrat Volcano
9. Brimstone Lake
10. Poopedcat Pass
11. Stinko Peak
12. Dark Forest
13. Vain Vampires Valley
14. Goose Bumps Gorge
15. The Shadow Line Pass
16. Penny Pincher Castle
17. Nature Reserve Park
18. Las Ratayas Marinas
19. Fossil Forest
20. Lake Lake
21. Lake Lakelake
22. Lake Lakelakelake
23. Cheddar Crag
24. Cannycat Castle
25. Valley of the Giant Sequoia
26. Cheddar Springs
27. Sulfurous Swamp
28. Old Reliable Geyser
29. Vole Vale
30. Ravingrat Ravine
31. Gnat Marshes
32. Munster Highlands
33. Mousehara Desert
34. Oasis of the Sweaty Camel
35. Cabbagehead Hill
36. Rattytrap Jungle
37. Rio Mosquito

Dear mouse friends,
Thanks for reading, and farewell
till the next book.
It'll be another whisker-licking-good
adventure, and that's a promise!

Geronimo Stilton